Kids love reading
Choose Your Own Adventure®!

"Adventurous, funny, sometimes terrifying; you haven't lived until you've read this book, so if you want to live, read it."

Ciera Fiaschetti, age 10

"If you don't read this book, you will, and I quote, 'get payback.'"

Amy Cook, age 10

"Warning: 99% chance of death. This book might make you cry."

Cody Curran, age 11

"Step in this book if you dare, but you better beware of what's inside here."

Gabe Frankel, age 10

CHECK OUT CHOOSE YOUR OWN NIGHTMARE:
EIGHTH GRADE WITCH
BLOOD ISLAND • SNAKE INVASION

YOU MIGHT ALSO ENJOY THESE BESTSELLERS...

CHOOSE YOUR OWN ADVENTURE®

PRISONER OF THE ANT PEOPLE

BY R. A. MONTGOMERY

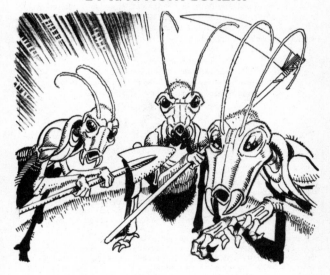

ILLUSTRATED BY JASON MILLET
COVER ILLUSTRATED BY J. DONPLOYPETCH

CHOOSECO

WAITSFIELD, VERMONT

Illustrated by Jason Millet
Cover Illustrated by J. Donploypetch
Book design by Stacey Boyd, Big Eyedea Visual Design
For information regarding permission, write to:

CHOOSECO
P.O. Box 46
Waitsfield, Vermont 05673
www.cyoa.com

Publisher's Cataloging-In-Publication Data
Names: Montgomery, R. A. | Millet, Jason, illustrator. |
Donploypetch, J. (Jintanan), 1981- illustrator.
Title: Prisoner of the Ant People / by R.A. Montgomery
; illustrated by Jason Millet ; cover illustrated by J.
Donploypetch.
Other Titles: Choose your own adventure ; 10.
Description: [Revised edition]. | Waitsfield, Vermont :
Chooseco, [2010] | Originally published: New York : Bantam
Books, ©1983. Choose your own adventure ; 25. | Summary: Your
mission with the Zondo Quest Group is to combat the Evil Power
Master who has reportedly allied with the Ant People. Are your
missing group members playing a prank or have the Ant People
taken them prisoner?
Identifiers: ISBN 1933390107 | ISBN 9781933390109
Subjects: LCSH: Human-alien encounters—Juvenile fiction.
| Missing persons—Juvenile fiction. | CYAC: Human-alien
encounters—Fiction. | Missing persons—Fiction. | LCGFT: Science
fiction. | Choose-your-own stories.
Classification: LCC PZ7.M7684 Pr 2010 | DDC [Fic]—dc23

Published simultaneously in the United States and Canada

Printed in Malaysia

18 17 16 15 14 13 12 11 10 9

To Anson and Ramsey

With special thanks to
Julius Goodman
for all his editorial
and writing help.

*And to Shannon,
Rebecca,
Avery and Lila*

BEWARE and WARNING!

This book is different from other books.

You and YOU ALONE are in charge of what happens in this story.

There are dangers, choices, adventures, and consequences. YOU must use all of your numerous talents and much of your enormous intelligence. The wrong decision could end in disaster—even death. But don't despair. At any time, YOU can go back and make another choice, alter the path of your story, and change its result.

You are a research miniaturization specialist in the Zondo Quest Group. Your mission: determine how the Evil Power Master has unlocked secrets of Universal energy so you may prevent him from causing the disintegration of matter. Flppto and Rendoxoll, two of your research team members, come to you with bad news: the Rimpoche and Baba Ram teams are both missing. Should you undergo miniaturization and go look for them? Or have they been kidnapped by the Evil Power Master?

You are sitting at home in your living sphere, a perfectly round, gravity-free structure. A hologram generator sits next to the entrance hatch, ready to be switched on. You can choose from 17,000 different environments, and for today you have decided on a villa in the Greek town of Minos in the third century B.C. You switch on the generator. Instantly you are there, or at least it seems as though you are. Your sphere is now a villa. You can hear voices in the street outside, and you can smell fresh thyme and wildflowers.

But just as you are about to relax in the villa, the hologram generator clicks off. You are back to your dull old white-walled sphere.

"Drat. What's up now?" you say.

The concealed speaker hisses, and then you hear the announcement.

"Emergency!

"Emergency!

"All Zondo Quest Group II members go immediately to command chamber. Repeat, immediately!"

You are out of your room and into the free-fall communication tube in seconds.

Turn to the next page.

2

You have been a member of Zondo Quest Group II for three years now. Your amazing talent with computers led you to the attention of this special group of researchers: a collection of the finest minds from Earth, Mars, and Planet F32, a planet at the outer rim of the galaxy. Planet F32 has a real name, but no one can pronounce it.

For seven years the Zondo Quest Group has been working around the clock in three shifts of three. The group's mission is to combat the Evil Power Master, an entity nobody knows much about, who is trying to destroy individual planets one by one. The Evil Power Master has unlocked some of the secrets of the universe and is able to cause the disintegration of matter. Everything crumbles as molecules break up and atoms fall apart—sometimes with devastating explosions.

The Zondo Quest Group is in overdrive to find out how the Evil Power Master is doing this and stop him or her or it. It's rumored that other groups of concerned beings are also on the trail of the Evil Power Master. You haven't run into them yet.

Turn to page 5.

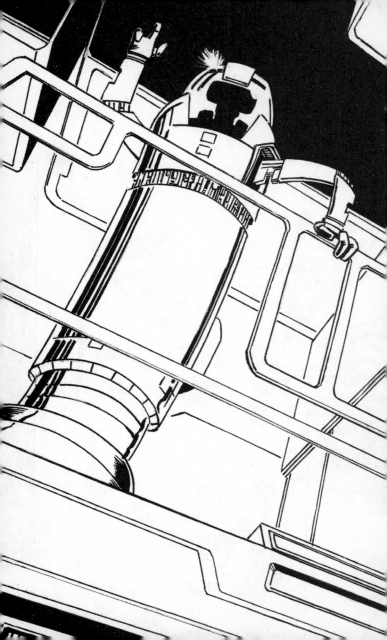

You were selected by the researchers to be trained in the Computer Organized Laser Miniaturization Program (COLMP). They wanted a young person to try new approaches. That's just fine with you, but it has been tough—very tough. There is no time for fun, only work followed by more work.

When you asked your group leader about it, Rendoxoll responded in its squeaky mechanical voice, "We must stop the Evil Power Master now! If we do not, there will be no—repeat, no—hope for any of us. All will disappear like smoke in the wind. We must get to the building blocks of the universe. Only then can we develop a plan to stop the Evil Power Master from tearing them apart. We must succeed."

It clanked several times and squished its soft plastic hands together. You weren't sure whether or not you believed this mechanical creature from F32, but at least you'd been given an answer.

Later you checked with your second teammate, Flppto, a Martian who is relatively earthlike. Flppto confirmed Rendoxoll's story. But he also said that he wouldn't really mind if entropy overcame the universe. "Personally, I'd find it interesting to break up into minute pieces. You'd never know what would happen!"

Turn to page 8.

6

"I'm with you, Rendoxoll," you say. "Lead the way. How about it, Flppto?"

Flppto nods his nicely-shaped head. Except for his lack of a nose and ears, he could almost pass for an Earthling. He gets oxygen through osmosis, and his entire skin surface is his hearing system, giving him the equivalent of hundreds of thousands of microphones. He often claims to be able to hear atoms clanging against each other, but his wildest claim is that he can hear thoughts before they are put into words.

You give a fleeting look at the communication tube that leads back to your comfortable little sphere. Then you join your two companions. The three of you pass by the mechanical guards and enter the research chamber by punching in a complex seventeen-digit code on the digital lock. (Your work on atomic structure is so top secret that you need both guards and mechanical security devices.)

Go on to the next page.

Click! The hatch opens. The research lab is silent and empty. On the desk near the laser miniaturizer are the remains of the Baba Ram Team's lunch. You look closely at the sandwich wrappers. No crumbs. That's strange!

Turn to page 10.

8

With a slight bounce you come to rest on the artificial grass of the research chamber. Rendoxoll hovers in the center of the room, emitting its usual orange glow. This time, though, it is a brighter orange than usual—almost a red. Its plastic flipper-like arms are quietly tucked away in its dull blue-and-green metallic shell. Flppto sits nearby in a foam-jelly chair. He calmly folds a piece of used computer printout into the shape of a spaceship and proceeds to toss it into the air with a smile. You can tell that Rendoxoll doesn't like such unprofessional behavior, but it ignores Flppto.

"Well, what's up?" you ask.

Rendoxoll swivels toward you and speaks.

"All members of the Rimpoche Team are missing. The Rimpoche Team members entered the research lab at the 000170 appointed phase but have not come out. They are gone."

You take a seat in another foam-jelly chair and lean back. "Oh, you know, they're Minervians. It's one of their games. They'll be back."

Rendoxoll bleeps loudly at you—its usual sign of annoyance.

"Security search reveals no hidden Minervians in the research chamber. They are gone!"

You look at Flppto. He grins. "Good riddance. They were pests."

"Stop, or I will have you demoted—you heap of protoplasm, you low-level air-breather!" Rendoxoll threatens between bleeps.

Turn to page 11.

"Well, let's go. Switch on the miniaturizer," you say. "They're not here—they must have miniaturized. I knew they'd get into trouble. It's still not safe to miniaturize to subatomic size. They were too eager."

Rendoxoll hesitates. "Wait, Earthling. Should we not search here first before the miniaturizer is turned on?"

If you say that the three of you should miniaturize immediately, turn to page 18.

If you agree and make a scan of the area, turn to page 34.

You know this must be trouble. Rendoxoll only says things like that when it's really annoyed. Now the robot continues speaking in its scratchy mechanical voice.

"The Baba Ram Team is also missing. Same conditions. I need volunteers to search for them. I will lead. Are you two with me? We will miniaturize and begin an atomic-ray search process."

If you agree to go with Rendoxoll, turn to page 6.

If you and Flppto decide to form a separate search team, turn to page 13.

If you suggest that you should keep watch in the research chamber while your teammates search, turn to page 15.

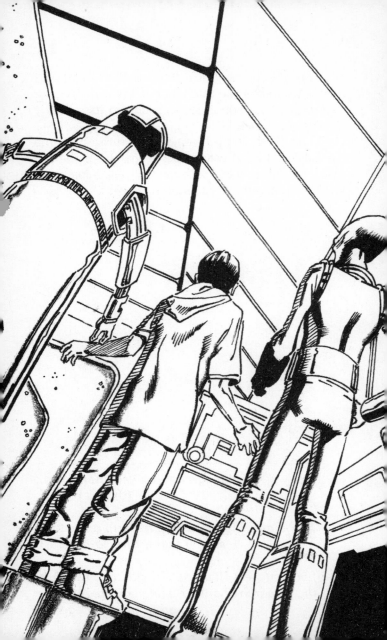

13

"Flppto and I work well together, Rendoxoll. Besides, it will be much better if we have two search teams. So you go your way, and we'll go ours."

Rendoxoll shudders slightly, a sure sign of its displeasure, but it agrees.

"Go then. Go on. You will be out of my way."

In the blink of an eye, Rendoxoll hits the miniaturizer button, and the three of you are instantly reduced, clothes and all, to the size of a grain of rice. The research chamber now looks like an enormous cavern glimmering with pale whitish light.

Rendoxoll rotates around on its axis to orient itself. Then it is gone in a clattering, whining huff.

Flppto moves over to the remains of the Baba Rams' lunch. There are greasy wrappers from the tuna salad sandwiches the Babas consider an exotic delicacy from the planet Earth.

"Hey, look at this!" Flppto points to a series of marks on the wrappers. They appear to have been made with a sharp instrument.

"Can you decode these marks?" asks Flppto. "It looks like a message."

If you think the marks are worth trying to decode, turn to the next page.

If you decide that the idea of decoding them is a waste of time, turn to page 35.

14

"I'll try to decode them," you say. You look very intently at the strange marks on the wrappers. It's not easy. The marks look like this:

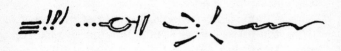

They might be marks from a fork, for all you know.

Then you remember a Martian symbol-game Flppto told you about—the most popular game on Mars, as popular as chess or checkers is on Earth. This looks strangely like that game, but oddly enough, Flppto doesn't recognize it.

Seven minutes later, though, you have decoded the message with his aid. It reads:

> We are in the grip of the
> Evil Power Master. HELP!
> Luzinia

Turn to page 48.

"Sorry, Rendoxoll, but I'm not going to volunteer. You know the rules yourself, but let me remind you of them:

"Zondo Quest Team, Article 5, Section 32, Paragraph 11. No condition ever warrants leaving the research room empty! There must be a team member on duty at all times, whether human or not—intelligence must be present."

Turn to page 74.

"Okay, I'll lead the way," you say. "Follow me— but be quiet, Flppto."

Inside the crack you see a series of tunnels leading off in several directions. The largest tunnel has a faint reddish glow. Another tunnel glows yellow, and a third glows with a white light.

"Well, which one, Flppto?"

"You choose, O Great Earthling. We Martians don't appreciate choice, you know."

If you choose the tunnel with the whitish glow, turn to page 68.

If you choose the tunnel with the yellowish glow, turn to page 70.

If you choose the tunnel with the reddish glow, turn to page 107.

18

Although miniaturizing is dangerous, you've learned that it is very useful in exploring the composition and structure of matter.

"We can't lose a minute, Rendoxoll," you say. "Time is crucial. They're not here. Let's miniaturize right now."

Flppto nods in agreement. You approach the glittering miniaturizer as cautiously as if it were alive. Carefully you position yourself on the round, red spot where the miniaturizing beam will be directed.

"Will you put the machine on automatic, Flppto? Thank you."

"A pleasure to be of service."

He hits the dark blue "automatic" square and joins you and Rendoxoll on the red spot.

There is a brief moment of calm. A shimmering golden vapor cloaks all three of you. It feels warm and relaxing.

When you look around, you are standing on a field of red rock surrounded by gigantic concrete cliffs. Towering above you is an enormous metallic object that casts shadows as far as you can see.

Turn to page 46.

You suddenly relax all your muscles and pretend to be unconscious. The ant carrying you does not even seem to notice.

This is bad—very bad. They probably don't want you for a prisoner—only a meal.

The ants carry you through a carefully carved tunnel. Its walls look almost sculpted. There is a reddish glow far ahead.

Finally the lead ant draws to a halt. So do the others. They exchange signals and then continue on, taking a branching tunnel to the right. It is dark in this tunnel—dark and damp. This tunnel is not as carefully carved as the other one.

The lead ant motions to your ant with his front pincers. You are dumped in a rectangular chamber off the tunnel. Its floor is rough, and its walls and roof are filled with what appear to be carvings. But they are not carvings. They are the dried remains of unlucky insects captured by the ants.

Will you be a meal too?

The End

"Help! Helppp...!" you cry. But it's too late. You are in Rendoxoll's power; so is Flppto.

Before your eyes, Rendoxoll begins to shed its plastic flippers. They drop off, and then the metallic body clanks to the floor. Before your terrified gaze, a giant warrior ant stands glaring at you.

The ant speaks. "Now you know. I am leader of the Ant People. It was child's play to take over the body of your comrade. We ants have been alive 80,000 times longer than Earthlings, and even longer than you Martians. We will rule the universe. We are more intelligent, harder-working, and more disciplined than any other creature. We are organized. We captured the Evil Power Master, and now he works for us—just as you two will."

You stare at the ant before you. What should you do?

If you plead with the ant to let you cooperate with the Ant People, turn to page 27.

If you use your powers of mental concentration to resist the hold of the purple beam, turn to page 33.

"I don't want to leave you, Flppto."

"You must. Think of the universe, of all the universes! The Zondo Quest is too important. Get going. Now!"

You race out of the chamber and down the tunnel, stopping just once to look back at Flppto's smiling face.

Years later, you remember your friend Flppto as you sit in the command chair of the Zondo Quest Team. The Evil Power Master has been stopped— at least for now.

"Flppto was one of the greatest Martians of all time," you say to each new group of research recruits.

The End

"I'm going on. So long, Martian."

Flppto looks at you with Martian sadness and waves once. You plunge on, searching for Luzinia and the others. But the anthill is a complex maze of tunnels and chambers. There is no light, and after hours of careful searching you are hopelessly lost, tired, and scared.

What is most frightening is that there is no life in this city under the ground—no life, only the terrible fear of the Evil Power Master. His force is fear, his rule is death. You can't escape.

The End

24

You decide to join the aphids in their rescue attempt. Somehow, though, in the rush to the upper corral, you are roughly pushed into a side tunnel by a bunch of zealous aphids. You hit the wall of the tunnel and are stunned for a few minutes. In the confusion, nobody notices, and you are left behind.

When you recover, you try to find the way out, but you cannot. You are lost forever in the maze of the anthill.

The End

26

"Your friend Flppto is right. You must be careful if you are to get out of the Kingdom of Zom alive."

You stop dead in your tracks. Who spoke? Where did the voice come from? What should you do?

"Let's get out of here while we can!" Flppto gasps. "We Martians have always been firm believers in survival. This is just too dangerous."

If you reject Flppto's advice and continue on, ignoring the voice, turn to page 23.

If you try to retreat, turn to page 85.

You speak in a low voice, choosing each word carefully.

"O Great Warrior Ant, I bow to you and your superior intelligence and power. Please let me, a humble Earthling, work for the Ant People. I'm a hard worker. I promise I'll be helpful."

The ant chuckles. He clicks on a communicator and crackles in ant language. Then he hits the miniaturizer button. Instantly you shrink to the size of an ant. Seventeen worker ants sweep you away.

You are now a prisoner of the Ant People.

The End

28

After what seems like hours of walking, you come out of the tunnel into an enormous chamber filled with digital control panels. They're being monitored by ants!

You are invited in by an ant welcoming party.

"Come in! Do come in! We have been waiting for you. It's about time."

Turn to page 69.

You do not volunteer. No one does. Rendoxoll becomes very angry and orders everyone and everything in the lab on 24-hour duty.

"Come on, Rendoxoll! Why don't you volunteer? We're tired of letting you push us around," you say angrily.

Rendoxoll bleeps several times and rotates in an uneven parabola.

"You are weak, Earthling. I will carry on alone— but only because I never give up."

You breathe a sigh of relief. You know Rendoxoll will calm down in a few days.

Now for some rest.

The End

You heave a sigh. "I'll volunteer."

Rendoxoll nods and leaves with Flppto and the others. The "automatic" switch on the miniaturizer clicks on. Rendoxoll forgot to turn it off.

Wham! You are back to ant size before you know it. Standing around you is a legion of warriors. You are recaptured!

The End

"No, I'm not going, Flppto. I'm staying with you."

So you and Flppto both become the decoys for the aphids in their rebellion against the ants.

The rebellion is successful, but you and Flppto are captured by the rear guard of the warrior ants. As prisoners of the ants, you will spend the rest of your natural lives in an ant laboratory. You keep trying, unsuccessfully, to develop an artificial "honeydew" to replace the aphid secretion prized by your ant captors.

The End

You draw all your energy up toward your forehead. You become as calm as you possibly can—as calm as a quiet pond in a forest.

You concentrate.

You concentrate on the ant.

You concentrate on the beam of purple light coming from the ant.

You concentrate on your strength, your will.

"Foolish Earthling! You cannot break the power of the Ant People. Your power is nothing compared to mine."

The ant's purple ray intensifies. You feel your muscles burn. Your body tightens like wet leather drying in the sun.

You increase your concentration even more.

Harder!

Stronger!

Intensify your mind power!

A calmness floods you. Your whole being strains to resist the purple beam.

Turn to page 45.

"Okay, Rendoxoll, I'll get the laser scanner," you say.

Before it can reply, you leave the research chamber and take a transport tube down to the supply room where the laser scanner is kept. Minutes later, you come back with the scanner, which sits snugly in its holster on your belt. You punch in the digits on the research chamber's lock.

The door clicks open.

"Hey, Flppto, I've got…" You stop in mid-sentence.

No one is there!

The guards say no one has left the chamber. They haven't seen or heard anything unusual, either.

If you decide to investigate the chamber, turn to page 41.

If you think you should stay out of the chamber, at least for now, turn to page 50.

"It's a waste of time, Flppto. I'm sure those are just fork marks. Let's get on with the search."

Flppto nods his head and scans the area, shading his eyes with a webbed, pebbly-skinned hand.

"Nothing! Nothing in sight. This feels like a vast, barren land."

You nod in agreement. You both feel lonely in this empty area. At that precise moment, you hear something.

"Quiet! Quiet, Flppto! Did you hear that?"

Flppto leans forward. "Of course, Earthling. I hear everything."

"Well, what is it then?"

Flppto scowls at you and answers, "Oh, it's elementary, quite elementary. That is humming. It's coming from an ant nursery. Probably slave or worker ants lulling the wee ones to sleep. What else do you want to know?"

You stare at Flppto.

"Flppto, Flppto, wake up! Maybe that's where they are. Maybe they're with the ants."

A voice invades the chamber. It seems to come from beneath your feet.

"You are quite correct. Your friends are prisoners of the Ant People. And so are you."

Turn to page 38.

"I can't leave Flppto alone. I'm going to search for him. You go ahead, Rendoxoll. We'll be along later."

You edge toward the entrance to the storehouse, brushing against several of the dried bugs hanging on the wall.

"You humanoids are all the same: too sentimental. Loyalty, sentiment—they have no place in the real universe. You are foolish. It is your choice, but if you go I think we will never meet again—at least in our present states."

"Thanks for nothing, Rendoxoll."

At that very moment the miniaturizer clicks on automatically. Rendoxoll is transformed before your eyes, growing larger by the second. You're growing, too. You and Rendoxoll burst through the ant tunnels as you regain your full size. Finally you are standing on the ground outside the Zondo Quest Center. Flppto emerges from the ground almost simultaneously. He grins.

"Just like a bunch of flowers poking our heads out of the ground. Yay, us!"

Rendoxoll swivels around sharply. "We are lucky that Flppto was so forgetful as to put the time-trigger on automatic—since I have told him never to do so without my permission."

Go on to the next page.

Flppto just smiles and brushes a few ants off his arm. The three of you return to the research center, ready to continue your search for the rest of the Zondo Quest Group. You look over at Rendoxoll. Unbelievably, you think you see a smile on its gleaming metallic face.

The End

38

At that instant a powerful paralyzing ray beams up from the ground. It freezes you and Flppto in your tracks. From all sides come worker and slave ants. They are just about your size, and they are terrifying.

"Look at those guys. Look at those jaws. We don't stand a chance!" you exclaim.

Once again the mysterious voice speaks.

"Quite right. It would be foolish to resist. One of your people—or, rather, one of your things, Rendoxoll by name, I believe—was foolish enough to resist. We took care of it."

A battalion of ants grabs you roughly and drags you off. You faint. Hours later, you awaken to find that you and Flppto have been tied up. You are leaning against the wall of a small chamber.

Turn to the next page.

40

"Good, you're awake," Flppto says. "I can untie these knots. What do you think—shall we try to escape now?"

"If we make a break for it now, we'll probably be recaptured. We haven't the faintest idea where we are."

"Yes, Earthling, you are right. You do surprise me with your powers of reason."

"You're sounding more like Rendoxoll every day, Flppto. Cut it out, will you?"

There is a pause.

"I'm hungry," Flppto says.

"Me too, Flppto, but that will have to wait."

You dream of Earth food. Pizza, scrambled eggs, cheeseburgers, even tuna sandwiches drift by in your imagination. Try as you might, you can't push the food out of your mind. You wish Flppto hadn't mentioned it, but then he was probably listening to your thoughts.

Finally you fall asleep.

Turn to page 72.

This is definitely weird—and scary. Rendoxoll and Flppto are gone. The other researchers are gone, too. You're the only one left.

One foot after another—slowly and with infinite patience—you walk into the miniaturizing room. The hatch door automatically closes the moment you leave its scan sector. The only sound is your breathing and the slight hiss of air being pumped into the chamber.

You notice that the time-trigger on the laser miniaturizer has been left on automatic. Who could have done that? Why would anyone do it? It is a hard-and-fast rule never to use the automatic miniaturizer sequence unless the entire Zondo Quest Team is in the miniaturizing room, all present and accounted for.

Before you can act, the laser miniaturizer snaps on, a beam of polarized light envelops you, the machine clicks off, and...

Turn to page 47.

42

You pick up the magnifying glass and realize that it holds a strange power. A laser-like beam shoots forth from the curved glass, cutting through the walls of the chamber to reveal tunnels and other chambers beyond. Some of the chambers are crammed with wheat and barley, flower petals, and edible roots. Other chambers are gigantic nurseries holding thousands of infant ants, all guarded and watched over by workers. In one chamber are hundreds of insects—aphids you think—which are being herded and milked by still other workers.

The beam of light hurts no ant. It seems to have a mind of its own. Finally, the laser beam of the magnifying glass pierces the walls of a small chamber.

There they are! Luzinia and the Zondo Quest Team all held tightly in the power of a pulsating ring of dark red light. You are sure the light must be the Evil Power Master.

You don't know how you'll overcome the Evil Power Master, but at least you know where to go now.

Good luck!

The End

44

The empty book seemed full of promise, but it is useless. Its blank pages seem to mock you. Without something to write with, you cannot use the book as a clue to tell others of your plight. Even if you could write something, how would you get the book out of the chamber?

You are captured by the Evil Power Master and never heard from again!

The End

Snap!

You did it. The purple ray is broken!

"Hurray for you, Earthling," Flppto cries out. "We Martians are every bit as powerful as you Earthlings, but I gave you the chance to show off."

"Not so quick, my friends. I have more in store for you." It is the leader of the Ant People speaking.

But before the ant has a chance to show what he "has in store," you leap to the wall and switch on the research chamber's sonic pest-eliminator. The ant is stunned and momentarily paralyzed.

The sonic pest-eliminator's frequency does not affect you or Flppto. Before the ant can recover, you have tipped him down the trash chute.

Now your only task is to find the Rimpoche and Baba Ram teams.

Good luck!

The End

Quickly you orient yourself. You were quite careful to bring along an accurate map of the research chamber, knowing that when you are miniaturized everything looks different.

"Hold on! Wait!" It is Flppto. "I can hear noises. They are coming from the west—from just about where the specimen cabinet is." He points over the hilly concrete wasteland that is the floor of the research chamber.

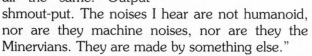

"Noises? What kind of noises? Be more precise, Flppto, or you will be removed from this team. You Martians are too vague."

"Oh, Rendoxoll, ease up," Flppto replies. "You machine types are all the same. Output shmout-put. The noises I hear are not humanoid, nor are they machine noises, nor are they the Minervians. They are made by something else."

"That information is not sufficient." Rendoxoll still sounds cross. "We must assemble all information input before taking action."

You intercede. "It's our only clue. Let's go ahead!"

If you decide to follow Rendoxoll's suggestion, turn to page 53.

If you decide to follow the noise, turn to page 63.

You are now the size of a bread crumb. In six more minutes, the automatic timer on the miniaturizer will reduce you by the same order of magnitude—to about the size of a virus!

You look at your watch and wonder if time has been miniaturized along with matter. You don't know.

Then you see them: three enormous creatures with shiny brown bodies, huge heads, fierce eyes, segmented chests, and pincers for hands. They are emitting squeaking, crackling sounds. They are headed right for you.

They are ants!

Before you can do anything, you have been captured. The lead ant picks you up in his pincer arms and passes you on to the second ant, who passes you to the third ant. All three ants seem to be making happy sounds.

You hope you're not their next meal.

If you give up and go with them as their prisoner, turn to page 19.

If you try to use the powerful laser scanner as a weapon, turn to page 60.

"The Evil Power Master again. I thought so!"
You puzzle over the note. Who could have written
it? Who is Luzinia? Then you see the body of a
worker ant crumpled up underneath one of the
sandwich wrappers. The ant is still alive, but barely.

With his dying breath, the ant whispers, "They went into the ants' Kingdom of Zom to help Luzinia in her fight against the Evil Power Master. I'm dying, but tell them I'll never forget."

With a shiver, the ant dies. You turn and stare at Flppto.

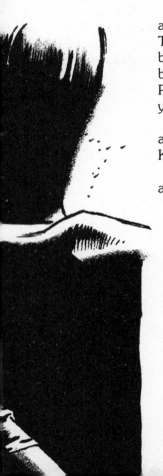

"The ants. I never thought about them. Who would have? They seem so insignificant. I'll bet they're the ones who have been on the trail of the Evil Power Master for hundreds of years!

"I'm game, Flppto. How about it? Shall we search for the Kingdom of Zom?"

Flppto reminds you that you are not armed.

If you hurry on to find the Kingdom of Zom, turn to page 73.

If you and Flppto decide to go back to full size and arm yourselves, turn to page 103.

50

You slam the door shut on the research chamber and lean against it, as if to keep out evil spirits.

You are completely on your own now. Of the three teams of three members each, only you are left.

Minutes tick by. Finally you push yourself away from the doorway and move about the room. The artificial grass feels strange beneath your feet.

Your immediate reaction is to go back home. You want out of this weird world of disappearing creatures.

Turn to page 56.

"Nothing to it, dear friends. Oh, pardon me, Rendoxoll—I know you don't like to get too personal. I just focused my listening senses and traced your breathing and speech patterns. Vibration-excavating did the rest. The ants are no match for a Martian! Well, let's get out of here."

"I'm with you, Flppto. How about you, Rendoxoll?"

"Not until we find the others. This is what I came here for."

Flppto shakes his head. "Not here. They are just not here. I've checked with all my sensory equipment. The Baba Ram and Rimpoche teams are not prisoners of the ants. They must have been super-miniaturized."

You and Rendoxoll stare at each other. You both join Flppto as he uses sound vibrations to excavate the floor of the research room. The miniaturizer should go on automatic and enlarge you in a few more hours. Now you must wait and hope that no more ants come wandering by.

The End

"I'm all in favor of doing this thing logically, okay?" you ask.

Rendoxoll nods. "You are one Earthling who has some sense. That is surprising. What is your plan?"

You pull out the map of the research chamber and lay it on a smooth part of the concrete floor. Then you kneel down and use your laser pencil to divide the paper into a grid of equal squares.

"I propose a search by grid. That way we'll cover the entire area."

Just as you finish drawing the grid, a shadow falls over you. When you look up, you see them.

You and your party are now surrounded by a group of ants. They look dangerous. There is no escape.

Turn to page 67.

54

"I'll listen to your plan, Rendoxoll, but I'm worried about Flppto. He'll never get out of here alive."

Rendoxoll turns to you. "You air-breathers talk always of being alive," it mutters in its mechanical tone. "It sounds so childish. I find you all very primitive."

"I heard that, Rendoxoll. I heard that, you heap of burned-out trash!"

"Yowee! It's Flppto! He's alive and well," you cry.

You spin around but don't see him.

"I'm here. Right under your feet."

With that, the earth moves and Flppto climbs out of a gaping hole in the floor of the storehouse.

Turn to page 51.

56

The guards in the room stare at their webbed feet, unwilling or unable to comment on the strange things going on. It is as if all the researchers have been eaten up, removed by the voracious appetite of the Evil Power Master. Not even crumbs are left!

You enter the communication tube and free-fall back to your room. On your way, you hear it. At first it is like a faint scratching. Then it grows louder and vastly louder. Now the noise sounds like mountains being torn apart or the thunder of tidal waves.

The sound increases exponentially. It doubles, doubles, doubles again, until…

WHAM!

Your universe tears apart. One last exploding, roaring, smacking blast of light is all there is.

The Evil Power Master has done it again.

The End

"I'm getting out of here," you tell the aphid. "We are pushing our luck too much. Sorry, my friend. You are on your own."

Flppto nods in agreement. The Babas back away from the warriors. The aphids rush in and immediately tie the warriors up. The four of you dash for freedom.

You make it. Flppto's sense of hearing guides you through the maze of ant tunnels back to the lab. You meet no more ants on the way; they must all be busy fighting the aphid rebellion. That evening, you are relaxing—normal size—in your own living quarters. Tomorrow you can get back to work on the Zondo Quest mission.

The End

"You can do what you want. I'm going back for Flppto," you say.

You dash for the tunnel. Three aphids are blocking the entrance. You push them aside and enter the darkness.

"Flppto! Hey, Flppto! Where are you?"

You are met by silence. Then you hear a faint cry for help. Five more aphids rush by. One of them is seriously wounded. The wounded aphid slips to the ground and gasps his last.

You plunge on deeper into the anthill. At last you come to the battlefield. Flppto is surrounded by six warrior ants. He is fighting for his life. All around him are dead aphids.

You lunge into the fray, kicking and swinging at the ants. Flppto shouts a greeting. He seems to be renewed by the very sight of you. With one final lunge, the two of you push through the warriors and race out of the tunnel.

A rear guard of aphids attacks the warriors, and the two of you make it to freedom.

That's enough of the ants. Back to work!

The End

60

The laser scanner is hooked to your belt. You twist in the ant's slippery grasp so you can reach it. The ant gazes at you with eyes that resemble a computer's intricate circuit board. It tightens its grasp.

"Yow! I can't breathe! I'm...agh...agh."

The ant seems to understand your plight. It loosens its grip immediately. You suck in the good air and squirm once again to reach your laser scanner. There it is. Grab onto it. Careful now! No jerky movements or the ant will notice.

The scanner is an awkward device, but quickly you slip it under your shirt until you can formulate a plan to use it.

By now, the lead ant has skirted the sandwich wrappers left by the members of the Baba Ram Team. He, or she, or it—whatever this ant may be—climbs down the side of the desk and proceeds across the floor.

Go on to the next page.

Down you go. It's terrifying, and even worse than your fear is the blood rushing to your head as you are held upside down. Finally you reach the floor. Now the lead ant seems to increase its speed.

In a seam of the curved wall there is a crack. The ant ducks its head and disappears into the crack. You never noticed the crack when you were full size.

The crack widens into a broad, dark tunnel. Then the tunnel ends, and you're astonished to find yourself outside, at the entrance to a large anthill. The lead ant is just disappearing into the anthill.

If you decide to go for a ride and see what's inside the anthill, turn to page 86.

If you think it's time to use the laser scanner as a weapon, turn to page 111.

62

"Easy does it!" you whisper. "We'll follow them and rescue Logo when it's safe."

"What do you mean by 'easy does it,' Earthling? Be more precise—like me. For instance, you should say, 'Proceed in total silence. Observe motion of patrol. Evaluate recapture possibilities. Execute plan when feasible.'"

You nod wearily at Rendoxoll. It always has to have the last word. Flppto stifles a yawn.

It is hard creeping through the craggy concrete, but you manage to keep hidden from the ants. Logo seems strangely at ease with his captors. His seven arm-like appendages are tucked casually into the rainbow-colored crystal tunic favored by the whole Rimpoche team. He wanders on as if out for a pleasant jaunt.

The faint sound of synthesizer music drifts toward you. Logo must be synthesizing!

Turn to page 80.

Flppto takes the lead, finding a path across the jagged, craggy concrete floor of the research center. You trip once and fall down. The concrete is sharp, and you are badly scratched. Rendoxoll notices the blood on your shins and beams a healing ray at you. On you go.

What would take seconds if you were your normal size takes hours in your miniaturized state.

"Stop! Be quiet!" Flppto holds up his hand. Rendoxoll bumps into you, and the two of you fall to the concrete with a thud and a clank.

"What is it, Flppto?"

"I don't know. I'm not sure, but I can hear a sound coming from there."

He points to a large tunnel-like opening in the wall of the research chamber. You realize that while the tunnel looks large now, it is really so small you'd never notice it if you were bigger.

"Let's go," says Flppto.

Before you have a chance to take another step, six warrior ants march from the tunnel. They walk in tight formation, at an angle to you. They form a perfect phalanx; if they were carrying shields, they would look like a Roman legion on patrol.

"Duck! Quick!" you hiss.

"Fine, but where to?" Flppto whispers back.

Flppto is right. There is no place to hide. The craggy concrete cliffs are no protection from this fast-moving patrol.

Turn to page 101.

"Attack! Attack! We are being attacked! All workers to tunnel entrance forty-six. Warriors outside! Repel attackers!"

The excited voice echoes throughout the tunnel. Another group dashes by. This group contains hundreds of large warriors, clearly bent on fighting to the death.

And—amazing to behold—right in back of the ants are Rendoxoll, the Babas, and the Rimpoche.

"Is that you, Rendoxoll?" you cry. You can't believe your eyes.

"Of course, Earthling. Use your eyes if you will, not your brain. And hurry. We are helping the ants. They told us of their dreaded enemies, the Sandozians—fierce ant-eating parasites. I said we could be useful in fighting them. Come join us."

For three gruesome hours you and the other Zondo Quest members help the ants fight the Sandozian forces. At last the Sandozians are defeated.

Victory is yours. Now you can go back to full size and return to your work.

The End

You head off across the floor, leaving Logo a prisoner of the ant legion. He will have to take care of himself for now.

The route you follow leads to a shiny metal tunnel. Rendoxoll enters without a second of hesitation, and you and Flppto follow.

Turn to page 28.

"We've had it. I know all about ants," you say. "These are scouts—warrior types out foraging for food. They'll eat anything."

"You forget, Earthling, that I am not edible. I am made of better things than mere protoplasm. I will handle this."

Rendoxoll suddenly spins in a high-speed arc, whirling toward the ants. But three of the ants suddenly rise up on their hind legs and spit out streams of gooey fluid.

"They've got me!" Rendoxoll squeaks.

Rendoxoll is coated with the gooey substance. Whatever the fluid is, it creeps into its shell, blocks its plastic arm cue, coats its optical sensors, and finally jams its communicator.

"So much for technology!" says Flppto. "We Martians have never believed in machines. It's you Earth-types who worship the things. Well, at least Rendoxoll will be quiet for a while."

The leader of the ant scouts approaches with the grace peculiar to the segmented creatures of his kind. Then he speaks.

"Do not be frightened. We will not hurt you. Please come with us."

Turn to page 113.

68

"I'd rather follow the white light. That red glow is too scary. Let's go, Flppto."

You are soon deep within the anthill. You see no other living creatures, but you come across chamber after chamber filled with the signs of what must have been a rich, flourishing civilization. You wonder if this was part of the Kingdom of Zom.

"What happened here?" you ask. "This place is like a tomb."

Flppto cautions you to be quiet. "You don't know who's around. We must be careful."

From far inside the anthill comes a booming, rumbling voice.

Turn to page 26.

They have been watching you through closed-circuit TV from the moment you entered the tunnel.

The speaking ant manages a graceful bow to the three of you, and then continues on. "This is an energy tracking station, part of a universe-wide network of energy watchers." The ant waves one leg at the bank of ants watching the hundreds of multicolored screens lining one wall. "You might say we are rather like your typical weather forecasters on the Earth-type planets. We check the flow of energy in the universe. We are trying to stop the Evil Power Master and his deadly game of cosmic checkers."

You blink at him as if blinking could help you understand.

"What good does it do to check energy flow?" you ask.

"Oh, come and see if you like. Join a search team." The ant gestures toward several ants in space suits standing by jettison tubes—which look almost like soda straws—waiting for takeoff. In each tube is a needle-shaped space probe vehicle.

If you choose not to join a search team, turn to page 77.

If you join a search team, turn to page 88.

You and Flppto creep out and follow the yellow light. The tunnel snakes back and forth like a river. Now and then you hear noises and see groups of worker ants in vast storage chambers or sleeping quarters. But luck is with you. You are not discovered.

Finally you come to the end of the tunnel. The yellowish glow is sunlight! The tunnel has led out of the Zondo Quest research chamber and through the anthill.

"We made it, Flppto! We made it! We're free."

He nods and moves out into the warmth of day, basking in the sunshine.

But you haven't forgotten your friends.

If you decide to rest in the sun for a short while and then go back and try to rescue them, turn to page 79.

If you decide to return to your normal size and then try to rescue your friends, turn to page 82.

72

You are awakened by noises.

Huddled next to Flppto are two members of the Baba Ram Team; it is dark in the chamber, but you can just make them out—translucent blobs on spindly legs. They are making squishing sounds that only Flppto can understand.

"Flppto, what's going on? Where did the Babas come from?"

"Shh! You're breaking my concentration. It's hard deciphering their squishes."

"Oh, come on, Flppto—what's up?"

Flppto moves over to you. "They say they escaped with the help of the aphids!"

You stare at him. "Aphids? What in the world are aphids doing here? By the way, what's an aphid, anyway?"

"You Earthlings should know! Aphids are pesky little insects that suck plant juices."

"Okay, okay, so you're a walking encyclopedia! So what do aphids have to do with ants? Ants aren't plants!"

Turn to page 75.

"We don't need to be armed, Flppto. We're a human and a Martian! Besides, it can't hurt to just look around. I say let's get to it. Where do we start?"

Flppto answers, "I suggest an ant hole. Where else?"

"Very good, Flppto, very good! You get a gold star for effort."

A careful search of the surrounding area reveals a small crack in the far wall. No light shines inside, and you sense danger. But this must be the entrance.

Turn to page 16.

74

Rendoxoll hisses like a teapot, swivels, and grimaces. Flppto emits a gurgle of delight at your performance, but he stifles it quickly. He's not eager to provoke this automated wizard further.

"Rules are made to be broken, Earthling. I am ordering you to come with me. This situation was not anticipated when the rules were written."

Rendoxoll activates the computer monitoring devices, extends an aerial that looks like an insect's antenna, and emits a purple ray that freezes both you and Flppto.

Turn to page 21.

Flppto smirks at you. "Ants keep herds of aphids, milking them for a honey-like substance."

"Oh, come on, Flppto, you've been reading too much science fiction. Ants are ants. They don't keep herds of aphids."

"They do, and what's more, they also have gardens. They raise grain crops and harvest them. They're probably smarter than you and your people."

"Okay, okay. But what's up now?"

"Well, the Babas tell me that the aphids are organizing a rebellion. They are tired of being used by these ants. They set the Babas free and directed them to us."

At that moment, Rendoxoll appears with the Rimpoches in tow. They are being led by an aphid.

"Time now to evacuate! Repeat, time now to evacuate. Return to the research chamber and de-miniaturize. This is a command."

If you obey Rendoxoll's command, turn to page 93.

If you disobey Rendoxoll's command and try to help the aphids with their revolt, turn to page 98.

"I'm for staying here," you say. "How about you two?"

Rendoxoll and Flppto both nod their heads in agreement. After all, your main job is to find the Babas and Rimpoches and get back to work in your lab.

"As director of research, I wish to inform you that your presence here is subject to review by the High Commander of Ants and his Board of Regents and High Chamberlains. We have taken care of ourselves for millennia. We do not know how to treat your visit."

This ant does not appear hostile, but he is firm. A legion of seven guard ants waits patiently behind him.

"We are interested in your work," you tell him. "Why haven't we heard of it before? There is no mention of ants and their energy-watching in any books or papers. No mention at all."

The ant leader nods his head. "It is a pity, but that is part of the sadness we experience. We have tried to communicate with you in many ways, but no one listens. No one ever has. Here we are, right under your noses, and yet you still don't listen."

Turn to page 92.

"What's that?" you ask the ant commander.

"Our sensors have picked up a heavy concentration of energy in Planet F32. We'll check it out."

The ant commander confers with his subordinates.

"Confirm. Confirm. Dangerous energy level in F32. Possibility of matter disintegration. Send warning. The Evil Power Master lurks."

You wish Rendoxoll was here.

"How much time until F32 disintegrates?"

The ant looks at you, shaking its head. "F32 is disintegrating right now. This very minute. We ants were originally inhabitants of a brilliant civilization. We were happily ruling our scrap of the universe when it disintegrated. It caught us by surprise. When our planet came apart our ancestors were scattered throughout space along with the meteorites. We've been working at trying to stop these giant explosions for millions of years. No luck yet!"

He speaks sadly, and you nod in sympathy. At that moment F32 explodes. A brilliant light suddenly illuminates the void.

You return with the ants to their home base. From now on you will try to aid them in their work—work identical to your own. You must save the worlds!

The End

"Ants! Who would believe it?" you say. "A bunch of ants! I've got to rest. I'm incredibly tired. Let's take five, and then we'll go back and get those creeps."

You stretch out in the sun, feeling relaxed and confident of victory. But you fall asleep without meaning to. When you wake up, the sun has set. It is dark, and Flppto is gone.

You are cold; you are hungry; you are scared.

If you wait until dawn before returning to the tunnel that runs through the anthill, turn to page 96.

If you return immediately to the anthill in search of your friend, turn to page 100.

80

Suddenly it dawns on you that Logo is not a prisoner. He, or she—you never have figured out whether Rimpochians are male or female— is actually the leader of this ant patrol. He is directing them; they follow his every command. They are his prisoners! At first you'd thought he was synthesizing—the Rimpochians' electronic form of humming—but now you realize that he is communicating with the ants. He is controlling them with some strange force.

"Could he be working for the Evil Power Master?" you ask Rendoxoll.

"It took you a long time to discover that, did it not, Earthling?" You glare at Rendoxoll, wishing it would blow a circuit in its communicator. For a moment you want to run up to Logo, but a feeling of caution holds you back.

Finally Logo's ant patrol joins the first patrol at the base of the miniaturizer. The ants latch on to each other, forming a movable ant-ladder. Logo scrambles up toward the miniaturizer.

He is heading for the control panel!

The orange control panel!

The panel that has never been used!

Turn to page 112.

Three hours later you and Flppto are normal size. You have taken two spades from the storehouse next to the Zondo Quest's research and living chambers.

"Okay, let's dig up the anthill!" Flppto says cheerfully.

Flppto bends over the spade, being careful not to crush any ants. He throws the dirt onto a screen the gardeners use to sift soil for planting.

"Hey, look!" he cries.

There in front of you are Rendoxoll, the Rimpoches, and the Babas. They are incredibly small, but they are alive and well. You are relieved that everyone can now return to work in the research chamber.

For a moment you have an impulse to tease the tiny Rendoxoll, but you resist.

Well done!

The End

The golden rope feels alive in your hands. You look more closely at it. It is turning into a chain of slave ants controlled by the Evil Power Master.

The rope winds around you and tightens. Your last conscious thought is, *Why, oh why, did I ever join the Zondo Quest Group?*

The End

Slowly and carefully you and Flppto creep back up the tunnel. Only the sounds of your feet in the tunnel can be heard.

"Fools! You can't escape from me!"

The rumbling voice surrounds you. You freeze in your tracks.

"You are finished! Finished!" The voice grows louder and louder until the entire anthill shudders. From above, a giant hand reaches down and lifts away the top of the anthill. Attached to the hand are the muscular arm and body of a well-formed humanoid. Then you catch sight of the face—it is the hideously twisted face of the Evil Power Master, ruler of the dark regions of the universe.

The End

86

You lie as quietly as possible, not moving a muscle and taking only shallow breaths. This is dangerous, but what an opportunity—a journey into the unknown world of the ant kingdom!

Your ant loosens its grip somewhat, and you are thankful for that. Then it carries you into the anthill and drops you to the ground.

All you can see are ants. The anthill is a storehouse, and you are being stored. The ant who brought you to this awful place is relieved by two smaller brown-red ants. They stand guard at the entrance to the tunnel. You collapse in a heap, tired and frightened.

You wake up several hours later. You're stiff and hungry. It takes several seconds to realize where you are, and that realization is terrifying. If only you could fall back to sleep and wake up later, safe and sound, in your living sphere.

"Psst! Pssssst!"

What is it? Who is it? you wonder. Then it comes again.

"Psst! Is that you, Earthling?"

It's Rendoxoll!

"Who do you think it is, the King of the Bug World?" you answer.

"Stop that, Earthling. That tone is not right for a member of the Zondo Quest Group. I will have to give you a severe reprimand. I repeat, reprimand, reprimand, reprimand!"

Go on to the next page.

"Rendoxoll, I'm sorry. I'm a little out of sorts. Where are you?" You can't believe it; you thought you were all alone in this frightening world.

"Remain calm. This place is interesting," Rendoxoll says. "I repeat, this is interesting, but it has not much to do with our mission of overcoming the Evil Power Master."

"How did you get here, Rendoxoll?"

There is a pause and a scratching sound. Then the wall on your left crumbles, revealing Rendoxoll, who has been scraping away with one of its plastic flippers.

"Oh, that stupid Flppto accidentally flipped the miniaturizer switch and *ZAP*—as you Earthlings are fond of saying—here we are."

"Well, what now, great and glorious leader?"

"I must remind you again—you puny, short-lived, fragile Earthling—do not take that jesting tone with me."

"Okay, I apologize. But what now? Where's Flppto?"

"Let Flppto take care of himself. I have a plan."

If you tell Rendoxoll you must search for Flppto, turn to page 36.

If you ask Rendoxoll about his plan, turn to page 54.

88

"I'm game. Let's go!" You can't resist exploration of any kind. Even your parents call you an "adventure junkie." You struggle into a space suit with difficulty, since it was made for ants.

"I will stay here," Rendoxoll says crossly. "You air-breathers take needless risks. Remember, we are trying to break the force of the Evil Power Master—not sightsee the cosmos."

"Hey, don't leave me behind," Flppto calls. "We Martians are every bit as curious as, and may I point out, probably braver than, your average Earthling."

The commander of the ant search team nods to Flppto, and soon he is suited up, too. He looks really funny. The empty tubes for the extra ant legs dangle loosely from his suit.

Flppto's voice comes over your helmet speaker. "If I look funny, you should see yourself."

The head ant interrupts. "This way. Take seats in the viewing module. Strap yourselves in. This is an extremely rapid hyperspace vehicle."

Turn to page 90.

90

With an enormous roar, your silver needle-shaped space pod is propelled into space through a vent tube that extends to the surface outside the lab.

The ant commander is precise and careful in his commands.

"Accelerate to departure velocity," he orders. "Decrease gravity device by factor forty-two. Bring space window into range."

The other ants are well-organized; they respond with speed and skill. The silver pod rushes through space, exits through a space window, and darts across the galaxy.

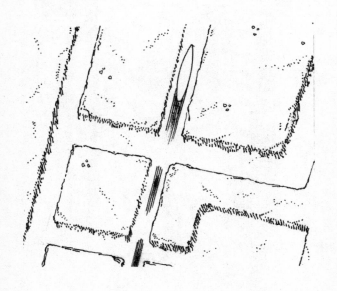

Go on to the next page.

"Where are we headed and why?" You have to know.

The ant commander turns to you. "Energy should be evenly distributed throughout the universe, but unfortunately, it isn't. The Evil Power Master disturbs the flow of energy. He destroys what he can, when he can. The Evil Power Master exploits any and all weakness! Some places have more, others less. We monitor these energy differences. We hope to warn planet systems in the galaxy when too much or too little energy is available. Then it is up to the planets to do what is needed. The trouble is that no one ever listens to us ants. It's frustrating."

You stare out the viewing port, watching worlds spin by in a blur of silver, orange, red, blue. Suddenly the space pod comes to what Earth-types would describe as a screeching halt.

Turn to page 78.

You feel the sadness in the ant's words and wish that you could make things right.

"Well, we're here now. We'll help. Just let us set up our research team. Together we'll beat the Power Master at his own game."

The ant leans toward you. "Perhaps. Perhaps. The Rimpoches and the Baba Rams said the same thing, but when it came down to it, they tried to order us around. You will do the same. We fixed them!" He smiles—an ant grimace that is terrifying.

"What do you mean? What did you do to them?"

The legion of seven ants moves in closer to the ant commander. He speaks. "They are our prisoners. We have work for them to do. Hard, hard work. It's about time we got some help down here. They are digging new tunnels and chambers for us. If you don't watch out, you will be doing the same. You are our prisoners."

"Hey, wait a minute! I'm with you guys—I mean, you ants. Let me help. I know a lot. I learn fast. I'll join you. I won't order you around. Come on! Please?"

Still babbling, you are led away and placed in a holding cell. Maybe the ants will relent and treat you as an equal. Then again, maybe they won't. Who knows?

The End

"You're right, as usual, Rendoxoll," you say glumly. "Our work is too important. We've done enough here. Let's get out."

The aphid commander looks angry, then sad. He opens his mouth several times, as if to speak. Finally he stammers, "Thank you, anyway." Rendoxoll brushes by him on its way out. You, the Babas, the Rimpoches, and Flppto follow down the tunnel. Twice you encounter a few ants, but with your numbers you can overcome them easily. You tie them up and continue on.

Finally you climb out of the last ant tunnel. You're standing in the lab.

"Hey, where is Flppto?" you ask. "Didn't he come with us?"

Rendoxoll scans the area. "Flppto is missing. That is too bad. We cannot wait for him. Prepare to de-miniaturize."

You want to go back after your Martian friend, but Rendoxoll is the leader. You know you should obey orders.

If you go back into the anthill to look for Flppto, turn to page 59.

If you follow orders, turn to page 114.

The ant draws closer and speaks in a low, defeated whisper.

"Some say the Evil Power Master will never give up until he destroys the universe. Others say all he really wants is fame. You can do nothing. Nothing. Do you hear?"

Ama scurries away. You are alone in the vast, empty chamber housing the ruby.

"It almost sounds as if she's been brainwashed, Flppto."

"Yes, you're right. Hey, what's this?" Flppto is standing in front of a table next to the ruby. On it are several objects:

A sword without a hilt.

A golden rope.

A magnifying glass.

An empty book—nothing but blank pages.

Go on to the next page.

There is also a note which reads:

THE EARTHLING MUST TAKE ONE
OF THESE OBJECTS AND LEAVE THE
ROOM OR I WILL DESTROY LUZINIA
(AND ANYTHING ELSE I CHOOSE).

SIGNED: THE MID-EVIL POWER MASTER
(SECOND-IN-COMMAND FOR THE EVIL
POWER MASTER)

P. S. YOU HAVE A CHANCE,
IF YOU ARE CLEVER.

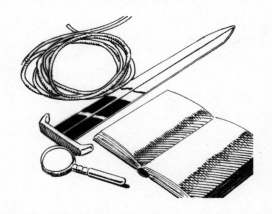

If you take the sword, turn to page 104.

If you take the rope, turn to page 83.

If you take the magnifying glass, turn to page 42.

If you take the blank book, turn to page 44.

96

You huddle up against a jumble of rocks and boulders, folding your arms around yourself to preserve what little body warmth you have. Now begins the long, cold wait for dawn.

Unfortunately for you, you made a serious mistake. At about three in the morning, a column of warrior ants returns from a foraging mission. They swarm over you, and when the sun finally rises, your bones glisten in the warm golden rays.

The End

"Too bad, Rendoxoll, but we're going to help the aphids. After all, they helped us."

Rendoxoll rotates at high speed, a sure sign of pure displeasure on its part.

"Duty above emotion, you-you-you…"

"Well, this seems like the proper duty. Right, Flppto?"

"But of course. On to the aphids."

Rendoxoll explodes in anger. "You weak creatures…you foolish lumps of protoplasm," it sputters. "I am forced to de-miniaturize alone. You will be sorry!"

It swivels around and glides away. The Rimpoches follow close behind without looking back.

The small green aphid now turns to you and Flppto.

"The ants are powerful, but they are too arrogant. We can defeat them. We need one of you to be a decoy and draw the warrior guard-ants away from the corral. Who will it be?"

*If you volunteer to be the decoy,
go on to the next page.*

*If you try to convince Flppto to be
the decoy, turn to page 108.*

"Okay! I'll go. What's the plan?"

The small green aphid motions to you to bend toward him. He whispers the plan into your ear.

"Follow me to the corral where the ants keep the aphids. Make some noise at the entrance to get the guards' attention, and then run for it. The guards will chase you, and the aphids will escape."

Flppto shakes his handsome head. "It won't work. I'm certain of it."

You and the aphid turn to Flppto. "Well, what do you suggest?"

Flppto ponders for several minutes. Then he begins a squishing conversation with the Babas.

"Okay. It's settled," he announces. "The Babas have volunteered to serve as an emergency support team. They will link tentacles and span the tunnel end with their soft, jellylike bodies. The ants hate the taste of Babas. We should have enough time to lead the aphids out of the anthill."

Turn to page 102.

100

That crazy Martian took off by himself. Well, I'd better find him, you think.

The tunnel is spooky, and fear races up and down you like lightning. Soon you are in the inner part of the anthill, where tunnels and rooms radiate in all directions.

Suddenly you are pressed against the tunnel wall by a stream of worker ants marching at top speed. Each ant carries sticks or twigs almost as big as its body. They are so busy that they never notice you. It's a strange feeling to be pushed up against a wall by these shiny, unseeing creatures.

Turn to page 64.

101

Then a second, larger patrol emerges from the opening. The leader of the Rimpoche Team, Logo, is walking with them! It looks as if he is a prisoner.

"Hey, Logo, over here—"

But you can't finish your call to him. Flppto clamps a hand over your mouth.

"Quiet!"

The marchers pass without appearing to notice you.

Rendoxoll squeaks quietly. "Logo does not appear to be in danger at present. We should investigate the tunnel."

If you decide to try to rescue Logo from the ants, turn to page 62.

If you decide to investigate the ant tunnel, turn to page 65.

Minutes later you, Flppto, the Babas, and the leader of the aphids are huddled together outside the entrance to a corral holding more than two hundred aphids.

"Shh! Shh! Here come the guards—on schedule. Look at those ants! They're mean," you whisper.

Flppto motions to the Babas to position themselves around the entrance to the corral. Then you and he step into the open space and begin yelling at the top of your voices.

"Ants go home!"

"Ants are cowards!"

"Down with ants!"

The ants rush furiously at you. You and Flppto step aside, and the Babas block the path of the four lead warrior ants.

"Come on, aphids!" you cry. "Let's get out of here! No time to lose!"

The leader of the aphids raises one leg in a signal for quiet.

"We must free the other aphids first. They are in another corral that's off a tunnel above here."

If you go with the aphid leader, turn to page 24.

If you insist on trying to escape now, turn to page 57.

You reach for the miniaturizer control, but you can't find it.

"Drat! Where could it be? You look, Flppto. It was right here in my pocket." Flppto peers into your jacket pocket, but he can't locate the control either.

"You must have dropped it, you clumsy Earthling."

"'Clumsy Earthling'? Why, you ear-skinned Martian, I'll have you know that we invented the word clumsy! I ought to know if I am or not, so there!"

"Impeccable logic, Earthling. Why don't you figure out what we should do now? I'm sure you'll come up with something good. As for me, I'm going to meditate on the problem." Flppto sits down on the ground.

When a Martian starts meditating, there's no telling when he'll stop. You're truly on your own now.

The End

You grasp the sword at the spot where the hilt was broken off.

"Yikes!" The jagged metal cuts into your flesh. Blood runs in a thin stream down your arm. The sword begins to glow. It leaves your grip, floats in the air, and speaks.

"Follow me. We will save Luzinia."

Before you can do anything, the sword darts through the air. It plunges down the tunnel into the anthill. Guided by the bright glow, you and Flppto follow.

WHOMP! You run into a force field—an invisible barrier in the middle of the tunnel. The sword hovers for a moment and then cuts through the force field. You and Flppto follow the sword.

After what seems like hours, you reach a room. In the center is a queen ant, bound and gagged.

She must be Luzinia. The Baba Team and the Rimpoches lie next to her, also bound and gagged.

Standing in front of them is the Evil Power Master—an ever-changing cloud figure of the darkest red. He gives a cry of rage when he spies the sword. The hiltless sword dashes at him, and the spell is broken! The dark red cloud dissolves into a mist. Soon it is completely gone. The Evil Power Master is defeated; Luzinia and her people are set free. The Rimpoches and Baba Rams are also freed and can return to work on the great task of the Zondo Quest Team.

Turn to page 106.

The last detail is Rendoxoll, but an ant patrol reports that it has spotted the group leader spinning about in a very busy and important fashion in a remote, lifeless section of the research chamber. It will return, you are certain.

Well, back to full size, back to work, and congratulations on a job well done!

The End

"Let's go. This must be the main tunnel. Careful! Quiet as sunlight, now."

The reddish glow seems to warm the tunnel as well as light it. The two of you creep down the tunnel. There is no trace of life.

Suddenly you hear a scuttling noise behind you. You turn to see a patrol of warrior ants dashing toward you. They pick you up and race off down the main tunnel.

Minutes later, you are in a huge central chamber. In the middle of the chamber is a giant ruby. Through a tiny hole in the roof of the chamber a beam of sunlight hits the ruby, producing the reddish glow that floods the room.

"Come in. You will not be hurt. You are members of a Zondo Quest Team, are you not?"

You stare at a medium-sized ant standing behind the ruby. It is difficult to tell the age of an ant. The ant's voice, however, has the sound of age and experience. You relax.

"Yes, we are from a Zondo Quest Team. Who are you?" you ask in turn.

Turn to page 110.

"Hey, Flppto, I would really like to be the decoy. But, Flppto, old boy, you are clearly the greatest. The best. I bow to you!"

Flppto turns to you.

"Do you really think so? I am rather amazing, aren't I? Come to think of it, I'm awesome in my many powers and talents."

Go on to the next page.

"Well, will you do it? Will you be the decoy, Flppto?"

"Yes, Earthling—but under one condition."

"What is the condition, Flppto?"

"It is that you must try to escape now and give up this dangerous game with the ants. The Zondo Quest Group needs you. I'm not half as good as you."

If you accept his condition, turn to page 22.

If you refuse and stay with him, turn to page 32.

110

The ant leans forward, bending her head nearer and speaking firmly.

"I am Ama, adviser to our queen, Luzinia— the greatest ant queen of all time. The fairest, the smartest, the kindest. This is her kingdom, the Kingdom of Zom. More than one million subjects live in our anthill. This is the largest, best organized, and most successful ant colony in history."

You look at Flppto and give a slight wink. This ant is either Luzinia's most dedicated follower or a public relations genius.

"Well, where is this Luzinia? And where are our friends, the Baba Ram Team and the Rimpoches?"

Ama points to the upper reaches of the chamber, where you see several tunnels. "Luzinia and your friends are all prisoners of the Evil Power Master."

Turn to page 94.

In one quick, smooth movement, you raise the laser scanner, press the trigger button, and sweep the area. The polarized light hits the lead ant in mid-step. Slowly he turns. A grimace of pain and hatred crosses his face.

You aim the laser at the second ant. He responds with a powerful emission of sound so loud and piercing that it actually blocks the photons in your laser beam. You never dreamed that a wall of sound could stop light!

Then the lead ant speaks. "Enough! We've had enough of your types stepping on us, poisoning us, filling in our anthills, flooding our homes, and destroying our kingdoms. Now it is our turn to retaliate—whenever we can.

"You will never escape. You will be a prisoner of the ants forever. You will join your friends, those who are still alive, in the tunnels and mines of our kingdom. You will work hard—very hard—for the rest of your life."

The End

112

Logo presses the control panel. Immediately he begins to glow in the brightest purple light you have ever seen. You stand transfixed, unable to move. Flppto too, is mesmerized by the scene. Only Rendoxoll keeps moving.

At first Rendoxoll creeps forward; then with a frenzied rush, it clanks up the ladder after Logo.

"Stop! Stop! You will disintegrate us all!" Rendoxoll calls. In its frenzy it almost sounds human.

Logo gives a musical laugh and reaches for the octagonal button on the control panel. No one has ever touched it, but it will switch on whenever a living being makes contact with it.

He touches it. *MMM_MMM_MMM_MMM_MM. ZURCHHH*.

The disintegrator has started to work.

Logo raises his head and shouts, "Revenge! Sweet revenge! I'm tired of you Zondo creeps. It's all over. Hurray for the Evil Power Master!"

The End

"There's nothing else to do. Let's go," you say.

Flppto nods. Whenever he can, he likes to copy Earthling gestures. One ant grabs the immobile Rendoxoll in its pincers and starts to drag it away. The rest of the ants form a phalanx around you, and together you march off. Along the route, you run into other scout parties and worker parties. Now you know why there were no crumbs left from the Baba Ram team's lunch!

Two warrior parties—you can tell them by their size and their ferocious look—are returning with the bodies of insects and other creatures unlucky enough to cross their path. These prizes of war are dead. Why aren't you and Flppto and Rendoxoll dead?

You leave the research chamber through a minute crack and finally arrive at the ant mound. The blazing sunlight hurts your eyes, but that doesn't last long. You are herded into the mound immediately. Before you stretches a maze of carefully connected tunnels off of which are rooms and chambers. In some you see piles of grain; in others you spy ants in egg and pupa stages; and in still others groups of workers. It is an entire city bubbling with constant activity.

Turn to page 115.

114

With a heavy heart you turn away from the tunnel and position yourself under the miniaturizer, ready to be returned to normal size.

At that very moment, Flppto emerges from the tunnel at full speed.

"Hey, wait for me! Wait for me! Can't a guy take a little time to look at the scenery?"

Minutes later, you are all back to normal size. You look dazedly around the research lab. *Was everything a dream?* you wonder.

Rendoxoll speaks. "Volunteers are needed to go on duty right now. We must not delay our research!"

If you keep quiet, turn to page 29.

If you volunteer, turn to page 31.

"Wait here." The leader of the ant patrol positions you, Flppto, and the frozen, gooey Rendoxoll outside a large chamber. You peer inside. There, before you, is a giant queen ant, terrifying and yet fascinating to behold. Around her are a bevy of lesser queens, workers, and a guard of warriors.

You listen to the ant leader.

"O Queen, Great Queen, we have presents for you."

"What are they? What's that?" the queen says. "One Earthling, one Martian, and one mechanical beast? Take them away. Put them in our slave colony. We will either use them or trade them, if anyone would ever want them. I can't be bothered with lower life forms like these."

The End

ABOUT THE ARTISTS

Illustrator: Jason Millet is a Chicago-based illustrator who has created storyboards and illustration for ad agencies, television, children's books, games and comics. His client list includes Disney, NBC-Universal, DC Comics, Archie Comics, Dark Horse Publishing and Major League Baseball. His work can be seen in the upcoming *Archie Vs Predator* from Archie/Dark Horse and on the hit TV show *Chicago Fire*.

Cover Artist: Jintanan Donploypetch.
Jintanan was born in September 1981 in Nakorn Pathom, Thailand and has just graduated from Faculty of Decorative Arts, Silpakorn University. During her studies, she collected numerous awards including "Best Animation" from the Thailand Animation Association. She has worked as an Art Designer at Kantana Animation House and is now an Artist at Tajkanit Partnership.

ABOUT THE AUTHOR

R. A. Montgomery attended Hopkins Grammar School, Williston-Northampton School and Williams College where he graduated in 1958. Montgomery was an adventurer all his life, climbing mountains in the Himalaya, skiing throughout Europe and scuba-diving wherever he could. His interests included education, macro-economics, geo-politics, mythology, history, mystery novels and music. He wrote his first interactive book, *Journey Under the Sea,* in 1976 and published it under the series name *The Adventures of You.* A few years later Bantam Books bought this book and gave Montgomery a contract for five more, to inaugurate their new children's publishing division. Bantam renamed the series *Choose Your Own Adventure* and a publishing phenomenon was born. The series has sold more than 260 million copies in over 40 languages.

For games, activities, and other fun stuff, or to write to Chooseco, visit us online at cyoa.com

The History of "Gamebooks"

Although the *Choose Your Own Adventure* series, first published in 1976, may be the best known example of interactive fiction, it was not the first.

In 1941, the legendary South American writer Jorge Luis Borges published *Examen de la obra de Herbert Quain* or *An Examination of the Work of Herbert Quain,* a short story that contained three parts and nine endings. He followed that with his better known work, *El jardín de senderos que se bifurcan,* or *The Garden of Forking Paths,* a novel about a writer lost in a garden maze that had multiple story lines and endings.

Jorge Luis Borges

More than 20 years later, in 1964, another famous South American writer, Julio Cortazar, published a novel called *Rayuela* or *Hopscotch.* This book was composed of 155 "chapters" and the reader could make their way through a number of different "novels" depending on choices they made. At the same time, French author Raymond Queneau wrote an interactive story entitled *Un conte à votre façon,* or *A Story As You Like It.*

Julio Cortazar

Early in the 1970s, a popular series for children called *Trackers* was published in the UK that contained multiple choices and endings. In 1976,

Journey Under the Sea,
1st Edition

R. A. Montgomery wrote and published the first interactive book for young adults: *Journey Under the Sea* under the series name *The Adventures of You*. This was changed to *Choose Your Own Adventure* by Bantam Books when they published this and five others to launch the series in 1979. The success of CYOA spawned many imitators and the term "gamebooks" came into use to refer to any books that utilized the second person "you" to tell a story using multiple choices and endings.

Montgomery said in an interview in 2013: "This wasn't traditional literature. The *New York Times* children's book reviewer called *Choose Your Own Adventure* a literary movement. Indeed it was. The most important thing for me has always been to get kids reading. It's not the format, it's not even the writing. The reading happened because kids were in the driver's seat. They were the mountain climber, they were the doctor, they were the deep-sea explorer. They made choices, and so they read. There were people who expressed the feeling that nonlinear literature wasn't 'normal.' But interactive books have a long history, going back 70 years."

Young R. A. Montgomery

Choose Your Own Adventure **Timeline**

1977 – R. A. Montgomery writes *Journey Under the Sea* under the pen name Robert Mountain. It is published by Vermont Crossroads Press along with the title *Sugar Cane Island* under the series name *The Adventures of You*.

1979 – Montgomery brings his book series to New York where it is rejected by 14 publishers before being purchased by Bantam Books for the brand new children's division. The new series is re-named *Choose Your Own Adventure*.

1980 – *Space and Beyond* initial sales are slow until Bantam seeds libraries across the U. S. with 100,000 free copies.

1983 – CYOA sales reach ten million units of the first 14 titles.

1984 – For a six week period, 9 spots of the top 15 books on the Waldenbooks Children's Bestsellers list belong to CYOA. *Choose* dominates the list throughout the 1980s.

1989 – Ten years after its original publication, over 150 CYOA titles have been published.

1990 – R. A. Montgomery publishes the *TRIO* series with Bantam, a six-book series that draws inspiration from future worlds in CYOA titles *Escape* and *Beyond Escape*.

1992 – ABC TV adapts Shannon Gilligan's CYOA title *The Case of the Silk King* as a made-for-TV movie. It is set in Thailand and stars Pat Morita, Soleil Moon Frye and Chad Allen.

1995 – A horror trend emerges in the children's book market, and Bantam launches *Choose Your Own Nightmare*, a series of shorter CYOA titles focused on creepy themes. The subseries is translated into several languages and converted to DVD and computer games.

1998 – Bantam licenses property from *Star Wars* to release *Choose Your Own Star Wars Adventures*. The 3-book series features traditional CYOA elements to place the reader in each of the existing *Star Wars* films and feature holograms on the covers.

2003 – With the series virtually out of print, the copyright licenses and the *Choose Your Own Adventure* trademark revert to R. A. Montgomery. He forms Chooseco LLC with Shannon Gilligan.

2005 – *Choose Your Own Adventure* is re-launched into the education market, with all new art and covers. Texts have been updated to reflect changes to technology and discoveries in archaeology and science.

2006 – Chooseco LLC, operating out of a renovated farmhouse in Waitsfield, Vermont, publishes the series for the North American retail market, shipping 900,000 copies in its first six months.

2008 – Chooseco publishes CYOA *The Golden Path*, a three volume epic for readers 10+, written by Anson Montgomery.

2008 – Poptropica and Chooseco partner to develop the first branded Poptropica island, "Nabooti Island" based on CYOA #4, *The Lost Jewels of Nabooti*.

2009 – *Choose Your Own Adventure* celebrates 30 years in print and releases two titles in partnership with WADA, the World Anti-Doping Agency, to emphasize fairness in sport.

2010 – Chooseco launches a new look for the classic books using special neon ink.

2011 – Reads of *Fabulous Terrible*, Chooseco's YA novel for girls, reach 1 million on Wattpad.com

2013 – Chooseco launches eBooks on Kindle and in the iBookstore with trackable maps and other bonus features. The project is briefly hung up when Apple has to rewrite its terms and conditions for publishers to create space for this innovative eBook type.

2014 – Brazil and Korea license publishing rights to the series. 20 foreign publishers currently distribute the series worldwide.

2014 – Beloved series founder R. A. Montgomery dies at age 78. He finishes his final book in the *Choose Your Own Adventure* series only weeks before.

2015 – Anson Montgomery's "lost title" original #185 *Escape from the Haunted Warehouse* receives glowing reviews from *People Magazine* and CBC Radio, and he is included with 24 other writers in the 2015 Twitter Fiction Festival.

THE
ABOMINABLE
SNOWMAN

CHOOSE FROM **28** ENDINGS!

BY R. A. MONTGOMERY

JOURNEY
UNDER THE SEA

CHOOSE
FROM 42
ENDINGS

BY R. A. MONTGOMERY

SPACE AND BEYOND

BY R. A. MONTGOMERY

THE LOST
JEWELS OF
NABOOTI

CHOOSE
FROM 38
ENDINGS!

BY R. A. MONTGOMERY

MYSTERY OF THE MAYA

CHOOSE FROM 39 ENDINGS!

BY R. A. MONTGOMERY

HOUSE OF DANGER

BY R. A. MONTGOMERY

RACE FOREVER

CHOOSE FROM 33 ENDINGS!

BY R. A. MONTGOMERY

ESCAPE

CHOOSE
FROM 27 ENDINGS

BY R. A. MONTGOMERY

LOST ON THE AMAZON

CHOOSE FROM 28 ENDINGS!

BY R. A. MONTGOMERY

PRISONER OF THE ANT PEOPLE

CHOOSE
FROM 28
ENDINGS!

BY R. A. MONTGOMERY

VITAL STATISTICS:

**PRISONER OF
THE ANT PEOPLE**

Friends on your team: **2**
Show-downs with the
Power Master: **5**
Ant People: **Hundreds**
Number of times the EPM
admits he's wrong: **Zero**

Ant People Trivia Quiz

Even if the Ant People have you imprisoned for life in their miniaturized colony, take a moment away from your worker status and answer these ten questions.

1) Who is the Zondo Quest Group up against?
A. A giant ant.
B. A radical group of political activists.
C. The Evil Power Master.
D. The Internet.

2) What does COLMP stand for?
A. Computer Over Large Mayonnaise Pickle.
B. Control Of Lions, Magic, and Puppies.
C. Cool Old Lemon Meringue Pies.
D. Computer Organized Laser Miniaturization Program.

3) Who is your group leader?
A. Rendoxoll
B. Randoxman
C. Flppto
D. Rimpoche

4) What does Flppto have that is far greater than that of a human?
A. Brain size
B. Shoe size
C. Appetite
D. Sense of hearing

5) What does Flppto claim to be able to hear?
A. The sound of the ocean, even when he is miles away.
B. The sound of your heart beating.
C. The sound of thoughts coming together.
D. The sound of planets rotating.

6) What kind of scary bug do you first meet when you shrink?
A. Cockroach
B. Ant
C. Butterfly
D. Ladybug

7) What weapon do you have to use against the ants?
A. Bow and arrow.
B. Butter knife.
C. Spear.
D. Laser scanner.

8) Who is Luzinia?
A. A member of your team.
B. The ant-queen.
C. The Evil Power Master's sister.
D. Your best friend.

9) Who is holding your friends and Luzinia prisoner?
A. The Evil Power Master.
B. Flppto.
C. The Martians.
D. The entire ant colony.

10) Which object from the table are you supposed to take?
A. The blank book.
B. The magnifying glass.
C. The golden rope.
D. The sword without a hilt.

1-C, 2-D, 3-A, 4-D, 5-C, 6-B, 7-D, 8-B, 9-A, 10-D

PRISONER OF THE ANT PEOPLE

This book is different from other books.

You and YOU ALONE are in charge of what happens in this story.

There are dangers, choices, adventures, and consequences. YOU must use all of your numerous talents and much of your enormous intelligence. The wrong decision could end in disaster—even death. But don't despair. At any time, YOU can go back and make another choice, alter the path of your story, and change its result.

You are a research miniaturization specialist in the Zondo Quest Group. Your mission: determine how the Evil Power Master has unlocked secrets of Universal energy so you may prevent him from causing the disintegration of matter. Flppto and Rendoxoll, two of your research team members, come to you with bad news: the Rimpoche and Baba Ram teams are both missing. Should you undergo miniaturization and go look for them? Or have they been kidnapped by the Evil Power Master?

VISIT US ONLINE AT CYOA.COM